ANIMAL DESIGNS TO COLOR

By Anne Hershenburgh

PRICE STERN SLOAN

Los Angeles

Cover design colored by Zaire Brown, age 12.

Copyright (c)1983, 1984, 1987 by Anne Hershenburgh
Published by Price Stern Sloan, Inc.
11150 Olympic Boulevard, Suite 650, Los Angeles, California 90064

ISBN 0-8431-1931-4

10 9 8 7 6 5 4 3

TIGER

PELICAN

MONKEY

GIRAFFES

KANGAROOS

CHICKENS

OSTRICH

SEA HORSE

OPOSSUM

FLAMINGO

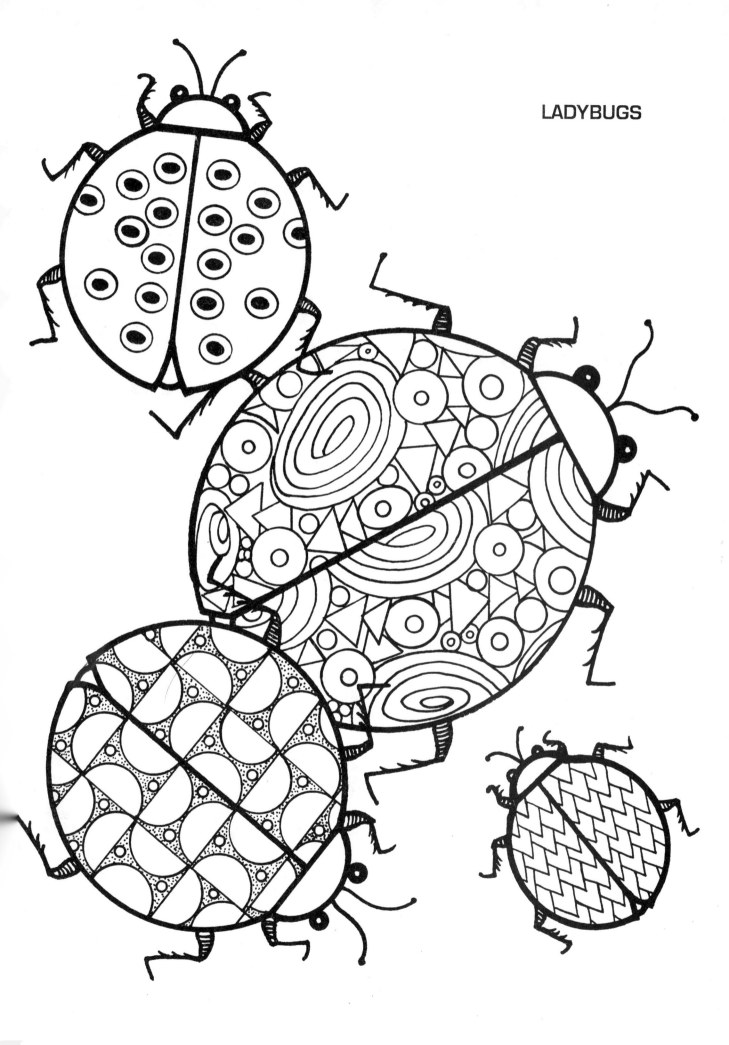

LADYBUGS

SEAL

GEESE

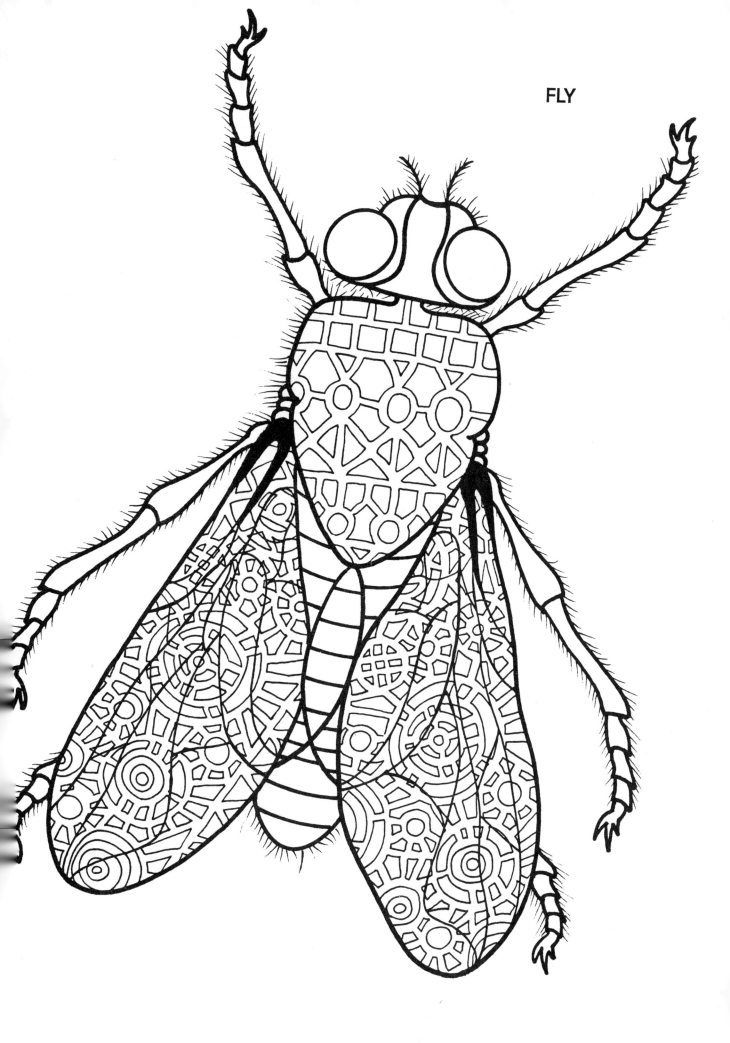

FLY

TURKEY

TIGER